Rupert
and the
Royal Hiccups

"I want to do something different," he said to his nephew Oliver. "So I've decided to give up magic. We'll leave this forest and live like ordinary people."

"Good! Let's go today," said Oliver, who had always wanted to travel. "But, Uncle Max, do you really know how to be an ordinary man? I've read books about ordinary people, and I think they're different from wizards."

"Oh, you and your books," said Maximilian. "I am the greatest wizard in the world. Surely I can get along in an ordinary place full of ordinary people."

Quickly, Oliver and Maximilian prepared for their trip. Oliver grabbed a box of peanut butter cookies. Maximilian combed his beard with a bat-tooth comb, then put on his traveling cape, his magician's hat, and his dragon-skin boots.

"Where's your magic ring?" Oliver asked.

"I *told* you," said the wizard, "I'm leaving it behind. I'm giving up magic."

So they left their castle and, after a long journey, found themselves on the main street of an ordinary town. In front of them was a red traffic light. "Oliver, you're always reading books," said the wizard. "What does that light mean?"

"I think we're supposed to wait until it turns green," said Oliver.

"Nonsense," said Maximilian. "I am the greatest wizard in the world, and no machine can tell me what to do." He stepped into the street.

12

"Uncle Max," shouted Oliver, "watch *out!*"

The wizard sprang out of the way just as a huge truck roared past. Its wheels splattered mud all over his cape and dragon-skin boots.

"You there," Maximilian shouted at the driver of the truck, "if I had my magic ring, I'd turn you into a frog!"

By that time Oliver and Maximilian had eaten all the peanut butter cookies and were getting hungry. In a bakery window they saw a sign that said TRY OUR DELICIOUS STRAWBERRY TARTS.

"What a kind invitation," said Maximilian. He hurried into the bakery, took several tarts from the shelf, and began eating them.

"Wait," said Oliver. "You aren't supposed to eat the tarts without paying for them. There are things called dollars and cents—"

"Nonsense!" said Maximilian. "I am the greatest wizard in the world, and I can read a simple sign. It says 'try our delicious strawberry tarts,' and that's all that I'm doing."

"But, Uncle Max," said Oliver wildly, "there are people called police officers—and I think I see one coming right now."

"Officer," shouted the baker, "arrest that man in the cape. He's stealing my tarts!"

Maximilian and Oliver fled through the back door. "What a town!" muttered the wizard. "I'd rather try to tame three dragons, five trolls, and eleven werewolves than try to live with these people!"

The police officer ran after them, shouting, "Stop, thief!"

"Quick, Oliver," panted the wizard as he ran. "Head for that little car—the one parked at the top of the hill. We'll escape in that."

"But you can't drive, Uncle."

"Nonsense! If I can drive a team of dragons, I can drive this little car." He got into the car and began pushing buttons and jerking the steering wheel from side to side.

"Hurry," said Oliver. "Here comes the policeman."

Without knowing what he was doing, Maximilian released the brake. The car began to roll down the hill, slowly at first but quickly gaining speed. Faster and faster it went, heading straight toward the mayor's house.

"Stop!" cried Oliver. "We'll crash!"

"Kerflam! Whomperoo!" shouted Maximilian.

But no magic words could stop the car. It crashed through the mayor's fence, rolled through his prize-winning tulip garden and landed with a huge splash in his Olympic-sized swimming pool.

People came running from all directions. "Help!" shouted the mayor. "There's a car in my swimming pool—and a strange man. He ruined my tulips."

"And ate my tarts!" cried the baker.

"And stole my car!" shouted somebody else. "Throw him in jail!"

"Glug! Splut!" Maximilian gasped, clinging to the mayor's favorite inner tube. "Swim, Oliver. Don't let them catch you!"

"But, Uncle Max," said Oliver, "there's something I should tell you." He held out his hand.

The wizard stared. "You're wearing my magic ring!" he exclaimed.

"I thought we might need it," said Oliver. "Are you annoyed with me?"

"Annoyed? Oliver, you're the joy of my life!" said the wizard. He seized the ring, placed it on his finger, and shouted, "Kerflam! Whomperoo!" He and Oliver vanished in a puff of purple smoke and reappeared in Maximilian's castle.

"Home!" said Oliver happily.

The wizard shivered in his wet clothes. "Now that I have my powers back," he said, "I'll turn everyone in that town into a frog!"

But Maximilian was too tired to turn even one person into a frog. Oliver gave him a glass of warm milk and put him to bed. For days afterward no one heard Maximilian M. Maxwell complain about being bored.

Aunt Connie's River Horse

By Eve Bunting

Kimberly brought in the letter from Aunt Connie. "Dear Kim," she read.

"In six weeks it will be June 3 and you will be ten. This year I am going to give you something different for your birthday."

Kim stopped reading. What did Aunt Connie mean, *this* year? Aunt Connie *always* gave something different. She traveled a lot, and last year she'd sent bongo drums from the West Indies. The year before she'd sent ostrich eggs from Africa. They were as big as grapefruits! How different could this present be? Kim read on.

"This year I am giving you a hippopotamus for your birthday. The hippopotamus, as you know, is sometimes called the river horse. Each one weighs over a ton and is about twelve feet long. That's about as long as a great white shark." Kim gulped. At least she wasn't *sending* a great white shark. Not this year.

"Hippopotamuses spend most of their days in water. At night they come out to feed. They like sugar-cane. Love, Aunt Connie. P.S. I'm going to be there for your birthday, too."

Kim put the letter back in its envelope.

"What did Aunt Connie say?" Kim's mom asked.

"She says she's giving me a hippopotamus for my birthday."

"Well, you can't keep it in the house," Mom said.

"The bathtub's not big enough," Kim agreed thoughtfully.

Dad said they should start preparing right away for the hippo's coming.

"We only have six weeks," he said.

The first week they planted fast-growing sugar-cane.

The second week they fenced the yard.

The third week they dug a pool.

The fourth week they laid the pipes and filled the pool.

The fifth week they built a hippo shelter with a palm-frond roof so the hippo would feel at home.

The sixth week they rested and watched their fast-growing sugarcane growing fast.

Dad baked a cake with ten candles. Mom made ice cream.

"We're ready," Kim said.

On her birthday morning, Kim got up early. She scanned the road and the fields and the sky. There was no telling how Aunt Connie would arrive. Perhaps on hippoback.

She came in a tiny yellow car. The trunk was too small to hold a hippo.

"Happy Birthday!" Aunt Connie shouted.

Kim didn't mean to be rude, but she didn't even say "Hello."

"Where's the hippo?" she asked.

Aunt Connie stared. "Did you think I was going to bring the hippo to you? Hop in. I'm taking you to the hippo."

"We're going to Africa?" Kim squeaked.

"No. To the zoo." She gave Kim an envelope. In it was a paper that said: *This is to certify that Kimberly Malloy is the adoptive parent of Hilda Hippo for the space of one year.*

"You have agreed to support her for one year," Aunt Connie said.

"Support her?" Kim imagined herself holding up about a ton of hippo.

Aunt Connie laughed. "That just means that I've paid for her food and care for one year—in your name. The zoo can use our help." She rubbed her chin. "I could have given you George, the giraffe. Or part of something. You can adopt two elephant legs or the front half of a lion. It's cheaper than the whole thing. But what would you do with two elephant legs anyway? I decided you'd rather have a whole hippo."

"Much rather." Kim pulled a photo of Hilda from the envelope. She stood chest-deep in water with an inner tube around her neck.

"Can't she swim?" Kim asked.

"Sure. That's just her favorite necklace."

Hilda was wearing the inner tube when they got to the hippo house. She had a garland of flowers on her head, too, for the occasion, and she bobbed up and down in the water, trying to knock it off.

"You're beautiful," Kim told the hippo.

Hilda let herself sink till her garland floated. Then she ate it.

Kim nodded. "Smart, too. I'm proud to have you for my adopted daughter. I'll come on the zoo bus and visit you every day. Pretty soon I'll be bringing you sugarcane, handpicked."

When they got home, Kim and Aunt Connie and Dad and Mom had ice cream and cake in the yard.

They swam in the new pool. The air was sweet with the smell of young sugarcane.

"I sure like the way you've fixed up the backyard," Aunt Connie said. "What with this and that, it looks as if you'll have a nice summer."

Kim thought about Hilda. What with that . . . and this . . . she knew she would.

BREWSTER ROOSTER
AND THE
THISTLE WHISTLE

By Dorothy Baughman

Brewster Rooster was bored. He walked from one end of the chicken yard to the other, grumbling. "I think I'll take a walk outside the chicken yard today," he said.

"You had better not," warned Harriet Hen. "Old Filbert Fox is always waiting for a chicken dinner."

"No silly fox is going to catch me," bragged Brewster.

"I warned you," said Harriet, and she went on scratching.

"Humph," snorted Brewster, "I'm not worried about that stupid fox."

Brewster squeezed through the gate and walked slowly toward the woods. He picked here and he scratched there. Suddenly, he noticed something moving in the bushes. It frightened the big rooster. He was not so brave now.

"I-I-I hope that isn't the fox," he whispered to himself. Brewster walked slowly away from the bushes. Out of the corner of his eye he saw Filbert's fuzzy tail through the greenery.

"Oh, dear me, it *is* the fox." Brewster walked faster. "I'll have to think of something to outsmart that fox. I can't outrun him now."

Brewster noticed something on the ground. It was an old whistle that the farmer's children had dropped. Brewster picked it up, but it was broken. It would not whistle.

"This won't do me any good," said Brewster. "I can't even scare him away with this. It doesn't make a sound."

Suddenly an idea hit him. Brewster smiled. "Maybe I can outsmart him with this after all."

"Aha, chicken. I've got you now," shouted Filbert, and he raced toward Brewster.

But the chicken had started some sort of strange dance, and he ignored the fox.

24

"What are you doing, you silly chicken? Be still, so I can eat you."

"I am dancing to the music of my thistle whistle."

"And just what is a thistle whistle?" the fox asked. "I have never heard of a thistle whistle."

Brewster stopped suddenly and said, "You have never heard of a thistle whistle? My poor fox, you are behind on the news. Thistle whistles are for very special animals, and I thought surely you would have heard of them. You are a member of the Animal Society, aren't you?"

"Of course," said the flustered fox. "I've been a member for years. I must have forgotten about the whistles." The fox did not want to appear stupid—especially in front of a chicken.

"Er, just what does a thistle whistle sound like? I seem to have forgotten that, too."

Brewster almost laughed out loud at this question, but he knew if he did not keep up his story, he would be Filbert's dinner.

"Well, you see, Mr. Fox, the thistle whistle has a soft, soothing sound, like the down of a thistle. That is where it gets its name, but it is so soft only special animals can hear it."

The chicken started his dance again. Round and round he danced. "Do you hear the beautiful music?"

Filbert did not hear a thing, but he told the rooster, "Yes, it is very lovely." He certainly did not want the chicken to think he was not special.

"Would you like to dance to the thistle whistle?"

"Why, yes, of course," the foolish fox answered.

Brewster handed the whistle to the fox and said, "Now dance swiftly in a circle, Mr. Fox."

The fox did as he was told, and in a few minutes he was as dizzy as a top.

"I can hardly dance anymore," he said. His head was spinning round and round.

"Oh, go on. You are doing wonderfully," said Brewster.

The fox kept dancing and finally fell in a heap, his poor head reeling.

Brewster started laughing. "You silly fox, there is no such thing as a thistle whistle," he called, and he ran and ran until he reached the chicken yard.

"The fox almost got you, didn't he?" said Harriet Hen.

"Almost," admitted Brewster, "but I outsmarted him." He told Harriet the tale.

"How funny it must have been to see a fox dancing to a silent tune," she said with a laugh.

"Thistle whistle!" Brewster laughed, but down inside he was still shaking. You can be sure he never took a walk outside the chicken yard again.

Bedtime
for the
Greenways

By Eileen Spinelli

Carrie, Irma, and Jen were three sisters who were quite kind to one another. Except at bedtime.

The sisters shared the same bed, and this caused a rumpus of cries and complaints in the Greenway household.

"Carrie's elbow is in my ear!" Irma would cry.

"Irma's cold feet are on my back!" Jen would yell.

"Jen is yawning in my face!" Carrie would holler.

Mrs. Greenway told them that as soon as their father

found a job, each sister would get her own bed.

Every day, the minute Mr. Greenway walked in the door, his daughters would surround him like noisy geese. "Did you get a job, Daddy? Did you? Did you?"

Mr. Greenway would wave them away and tell them that jobs didn't grow on trees, and that when *he* was a boy, he shared a bed with nine brothers.

Whenever he said that, Mrs. Greenway would tweak Mr. Greenway's mustache and say, "My, *that* bed must be in the *Guinness Book of World Records.*"

Mr. Greenway would grumble and say, "What about supper?"

The three girls would jump up and down and say, "What about our beds?"

And Mrs. Greenway would hold her ears and say, "What about some peace and quiet around here?"

One day Carrie got an idea. "Let's divide the bed into three equal parts with string," she said.

So Mr. Greenway went down to the basement for a hammer, some nails, a ruler, and string. He divided the bed. Equally.

At bedtime he read the girls a story. Mrs. Greenway tucked them in, each sister in her own space.

Scarcely had their parents closed the door when the girls discovered that string doesn't make very good fences.

Irma squealed. "Carrie's nose is on my side of the string."

Jen hollered. "Irma sneezed her germs into my space."

Carrie cried out. "Jen's staring at me."

One day Irma got an idea. "Let's all go to bed at different times," she said.

So Mrs. Greenway wrote three different bedtimes on three pieces of paper and dropped them into a hat. Each sister pulled out a bedtime.

That night Irma went to bed first. Her mother hummed her a song. Her father kissed her on the forehead. Good-night.

Fifteen minutes later it was Carrie's turn.

Irma wailed. "Carrie plopped on the bed and woke me up!"

Mrs. Greenway settled both girls and hummed them to sleep. In the meantime Jen had fallen asleep on the sofa. Mr. Greenway carried her upstairs and laid her as delicately as an egg in the bed.

Mother and Father were tiptoeing down the stairs when Carrie called to them. "Jen won't stop snoring!"

Jen woke up to announce that Irma's grinding teeth were giving her nightmares.

One day Jen got an idea. "Let's wear earplugs and night masks," she said.

So that night Mrs. Greenway helped the girls with their earplugs. Mr. Greenway put on their masks.

But even before her parents had reached the doorway, Irma pinched her nose. "Carrie's wearing her dirty socks to bed!"

Jen tattled. "Irma didn't brush her teeth. She's breathing on me."

Carrie sniffed. "I smell peppermint. Jen sneaked chewing gum into bed."

Then one day Mr. Greenway found a job.

The whole family celebrated. First by going out for double-dip ice-cream cones. Then came a trip to the furniture store. The salesman sold Mr. Greenway three small cots and promised delivery the next morning.

Mrs. Greenway decided they would keep the girls' big bed for when Grandmother visited.

When the delivery truck came, furniture men brought in the cots, carried them upstairs, and set each one against a different wall in the bedroom.

All day each sister bounced on her own bed. Each fluffed her own pillow, arranged her own stuffed animals, and folded and refolded her own blanket.

The moment the moon appeared, Irma yawned. "I think I'll go to bed."

Carrie stretched. "I'm feeling very tired."

Jen rubbed her eyes. "I feel sleepy, too."

Quietly, with no bickering, the Greenway girls washed their faces, brushed their teeth, and said their prayers. Then each sister climbed into her very own bed.

Irma sighed. "Terrific!"

Jen grinned. "Plenty of room!"

Carrie chirped. "So comfy!"

"My mattress is like a cloud," said Irma.

"Mine is soft as cotton candy," said Jen.

Carrie laughed. "I'm sinking into a tub full of bubbles!"

For about two minutes, all was silent.

Then Irma whispered. "I feel cold and shivery."

"I feel lonely," sniffled Jen.

Another minute of silence.

Carrie whispered. "Our old bed is for when Grandmother comes."

"Right," said Irma.

"Well," said Carrie, "suppose Grandmother came tonight?"

"Just suppose," said Jen.

"Well," said Carrie, "wouldn't it be awful if Grandmother had to climb into a cold bed?"

"Those sheets get awfully cold," said Jen.

Irma shivered. "Brrrr."

"I think somebody ought to keep Grandmother's bed warm for her," suggested Carrie.

"Somebody ought to," said Jen.

"Somebody," agreed Irma.

Carrie sat up. "I think *we* are just the ones to do it!"

Just five seconds later, the Greenway girls were right back where they started. In the big bed.

Only this time, no one was complaining.

Archibald and Me

By Penny Volin

It started the day the little kid with the stocking cap raced past me carrying a bowl of cereal and saying, "Gleep, gleep. Zorko."

Later I asked my mom who the weird little kid was that had zoomed out of our backyard.

She said, "That's probably one of our new neighbors. They moved in next door while you were at camp last week. And it isn't nice to call him weird. I'm sure he's a very nice little boy."

"Well, I bet you'd say I was weird if I were wearing a stocking cap when it's eighty degrees outside."

That got her attention for a minute, but still she said, "He's only four. You be nice to him. There aren't any little children in the neighborhood for him to play with."

I said sure and forgot about it. After all, it wasn't like I was going to be best buddies with some four-year-old.

The next morning I took my dog, Shag, out into the backyard for a run. All of a sudden this strange little voice right over my head said, "Hi." I'm not exactly the jumpy type, but that made my skin crawl. Shag started barking. It was the kid again. I guess his voice sounded strange because he was dangling by his knees from my old tree fort. I was beginning to think his mother should keep him on a leash.

I said, "I think you'd better get down from there."

"Why?"

"You might get hurt," I said.

"No I won't."

"Well, you're spilling your cereal."

"I don't care."

I wasn't getting anywhere. I didn't really care if he stayed there or not, but the way things go, I'd get the blame if he got hurt.

I said, "What's your name?"

"Archibald."

"Hey, Archie, if you come down from there, I'll let you pet my dog, Shag."

That got him moving. He was afraid to climb

34

back down the ladder, though, so I reached up and swung him down.

He said, "You sure are strong."

I pretended to be a strong man and used him for weight lifting. He went all giggly over that. He thought Shag was great, too. I admit it—Shag and I showed off a little for him. I figure it doesn't hurt to be appreciated once in a while.

That was my first mistake. After that, every time I stepped outside my house Archie seemed to be looking out his bedroom window. Then he'd either come tearing outside or throw open his window and yell, "Where are you going?" The kid would have been great working for the FBI.

And then there was Saturday morning. Saturdays I get to sleep as long as I want to. That's what I was doing until Archie showed up at my house. He wanted to watch cartoons with me. My mom was sure I wouldn't want to "disappoint my little friend," so there I was watching Saturday cartoons. Archie climbed onto my lap and said, "This is fun, huh?"

Actually, it wasn't too bad. Some of those cartoons were kind of fun. Archie would just chuckle and chuckle. Besides, this way my mom couldn't ask me to do chores, because I was already busy with Archie.

Well, it wasn't too long before Archie's mom decided I was the perfect one to baby-sit for Archie. I told her I didn't know anything about baby-sitting and I thought she might want someone older. But she was sure I would be just right. I finally agreed to take care of him a couple of afternoons a week. That was OK, too. I mean it wasn't like baby-sitting a baby. Archie thought everything was a big deal—like hiking, finding bugs, building sand forts, looking at my stamp collection, reading comic books.

It wasn't exactly perfect all the time. There was the day Archie covered himself with green finger paint so he'd look like a frog, or the day he rolled in the mud and played the mud monster. He did a lot of goofy things like that, but the summer went fast, and I earned enough extra money to buy my new ten-speed.

I'm pretty busy now with school and playing ball, but Archie and I still pal around together. Archie will be all right if he sticks with me. After all, he must be an OK kid—my Mom keeps saying he's just like me when I was a little kid.

The Forgetful King

By Jean Tullett Read

Long ago, in a land far across the ocean, there lived a king who was known as The Forgetful King.

He was a kind king and much loved by all his people, but he was always forgetting things. The queen and the five princesses were very worried because the king seemed to be getting more and more forgetful.

One Monday the king was supposed to talk to his people from the balcony of the palace and ask them to work very hard to harvest the crops while they were ripe. But the king forgot what he was supposed to say to the people. "Maybe I was supposed to grant them a holiday," the king said to himself. So he announced a holiday. The people cheered and went away and enjoyed their holiday. But that night it rained, and some of the crops were spoiled.

The king was angry when he saw his mistake and said to himself, "I must not be so forgetful."

But on Wednesday, when the third princess was to be married, the king forgot all about the wedding and went fishing. When the queen discovered he was missing, she sent the royal pages to look for him. They found the king fishing by a river. There was no time for the king to change, so he wore his fishing hat instead of his crown to the third princess's wedding. The king felt silly and said to himself, "I must not be so forgetful."

But on Friday, when the king was supposed to pay his servants, he forgot where he had hidden the key to his money chest. His royal pages searched all day throughout the palace, and finally, when night fell, they found the key hidden in one of the king's golden slippers. Again the king said to himself, "I must not be so forgetful."

But on Saturday the king forgot it was the queen's birthday, and she was very sad.

"This is awful!" said the king. He gathered his three ministers and asked them if they knew how he could stop being so forgetful.

The first minister said that the king should stand on his head for an hour each day to improve his circulation. The second minister said that the king should get more sleep. And the third minister said the king needed to drink more milk.

So, for one week, the king did what his ministers suggested. He stood on his head for an hour each day; he slept until noon; and he drank lots of milk. But he was still forgetful.

Finally the queen suggested that the king offer a large reward to anyone who could help him stop being so forgetful.

Each day crowds of people gathered outside the palace. But though the king saw each of them, not one person was able to help the king stop being so forgetful.

A week went by. One morning the king woke early and paced through the halls of the palace, trying to think of an answer to his problem.

The king saw the baker's boy carrying a huge tray of jam tarts, loaves of bread, pies, and muffins into the palace. The jam tarts looked so good that the king went down to the kitchen to get one. As he reached the kitchen door, he heard the baker's boy saying to the royal cook, "Here are the twenty jam tarts you asked for, the ten loaves of bread, the three cherry pies, the strawberry pie, the two peach pies, and the thirty muffins."

The king was amazed. He pushed open the door and commanded, "Quick, young man—tell me how you manage not to forget how many tarts, loaves, pies, and muffins my cook has asked for."

The baker's boy was a little scared. But he knew the king was a kind king, so he bowed low and held out a small slate and a piece of chalk. "I write what the cook has asked me to bring on this slate, Your Majesty, so I won't forget," he said.

The king was astounded. "You write it all on your slate so you won't forget?"

The baker's boy nodded.

"That's it!" exclaimed the king. "Why didn't I think of that? All I have to do is write things down, and then I won't forget them."

The king took the boy's arm. "Come with me, boy. There is a large reward for you because you have solved my problem. And I am going to make you a special royal scribe. You shall carry your slate and chalk around and write down those things that I must not forget."

And that is how the baker's boy became a royal scribe and how The Forgetful King never forgot anything again.

Morgan Ferrigan Fell into the Well Again

By Jill E. Rybka-Steelman

"Morgan Ferrigan, you fell into the well again!" yelled little Billy Joe Pruitt. He was looking into the old wishing well on his grandfather's farm, but all he could see down there was blackness.

"Morgan Ferrigan! You fell into the well again," Billy Joe yelled louder.

"Cock-a-doodle-doo!" Morgan Ferrigan cried. Morgan Ferrigan, of course, was a rooster. But he was so far down in the well that by the time his voice reached the top, his "Cock-a-doodle-doo" sounded more like "Cock-a-dawdle-daw!" It made Billy Joe giggle.

Just then a very old man passed by and saw Billy Joe leaning over the well.

"Whatever are you looking at?" asked the very old man in his very old voice.

Billy Joe looked up. "Morgan Ferrigan fell into the well again," he said.

"What?" said the very old man. "Speak up, please. I don't hear so well anymore."

"MORGAN FERRIGAN FELL INTO THE WELL AGAIN!" shouted Billy Joe.

"Who is Morgan Ferrigan?" asked the very old man.

"Morgan Ferrigan is my friend," Billy Joe said in a loud voice.

"Oh my. I hope your friend isn't hurt," said the very old man. He hobbled over to the well.

"I say! You in the well! Are you all right?" he yelled as loudly as he could.

"Cock-a-dawdle-daw!" cried Morgan Ferrigan from way down deep in the well.

"Oh my," said the very old man. "He said he can't climb up the wall."

Billy Joe was surprised. "You mean you can understand him?" he asked.

"I may be hard of hearing, son, but I'm not deaf," said the very old man. "I heard him quite plainly. He said, 'I can't climb up the wall.'"

"Cock-a-dawdle-daw!" cried Morgan Ferrigan.

"See?" said the very old man. "He said it again. 'I can't climb up the wall.'"

Just then one of Grandpa Pruitt's neighbors walked up to the well. "What's going on here?" he asked.

"Morgan Ferrigan fell into the well again," said Billy Joe.

"Morgan Ferrigan can't climb up the wall," added the very old man.

"Who is Morgan Ferrigan?" asked the neighbor.

"Morgan Ferrigan is my friend," said Billy Joe.

"Oh my," shouted the neighbor. "Little children should never play on something as dangerous as this old wishing well!"

"I know," agreed Billy Joe. "I would never do such a silly thing. I could get hurt."

"Right," said the neighbor. "It's too bad Morgan Ferrigan doesn't have as much sense as you do."

Just then the neighbor's wife came over. "What's all the excitement?" she asked.

"This boy's friend Morgan Ferrigan fell into the well again," said the neighbor.

"Morgan Ferrigan can't climb up the wall," said the very old man.

"Oh no," cried the neighbor's wife. "I must call for help. The fire department. The police. An ambulance." She ran away, shouting to Billy Joe, "Tell your friend Morgan Ferrigan that help is on the way!"

Before long, a whole crowd had gathered—

neighbors, delivery persons, even passing motorists. Everyone was running to the well.

"What's going on?" each one asked.

And Billy Joe said, "Morgan Ferrigan fell into the well again."

And everyone else explained, "Morgan Ferrigan can't climb up the wall."

The fire department arrived. The police came to restore some order. An ambulance pulled up, ready to whisk Morgan Ferrigan away to the hospital.

A television news reporter and a cameraman came. They headed straight for little Billy Joe Pruitt.

"We're here, reporting live from Grandpa Pruitt's farm, talking with his grandson, Billy Joe," said the reporter. "Someone here has fallen into a deep old well. Billy Joe, can you tell us what happened?"

"Morgan Ferrigan fell into the well again," said Billy Joe.

"Morgan Ferrigan can't climb up the wall!" shouted the crowd. They wanted to be on television, too.

"My, that's terrible," said the reporter. "He must have taken quite a fall."

Just then Billy Joe's grandfather hurried up to the well. "What on earth is going on here?" he shouted above the sirens.

"Morgan Ferrigan fell into the well again," answered Billy Joe.

"Morgan Ferrigan can't climb up the wall!" shouted

the crowd.

"So?" said Grandpa Pruitt. "Morgan Ferrigan falls into the well a couple of times a week!"

"You mean this isn't the first time you let a little child play on this rickety old well?" asked the reporter. Everyone was shocked.

Grandpa Pruitt laughed. He laughed long and hard. "Morgan Ferrigan isn't a child!" he said.

The crowd gasped. The fire fighters stopped their rescue effort. The police turned off their sirens, and the news reporter's face turned extremely red. "What did you say?" the reporter asked.

"Morgan Ferrigan is not a child," repeated Grandpa Pruitt.

The news reporter gulped. "Who *is* Morgan Ferrigan then?" he asked.

Just then Morgan Ferrigan cried out, "Cock-a-dawdle-daw!" He flew straight up and perched on the top of the well. The crowd was speechless. The news reporter's face went from red to white. But Billy Joe just smiled.

"Morgan Ferrigan!" he said. "You flew out of the well again."

The Glacier
That Almost Ate Main Street

By Gene Twaronite

It all started with the refrigerator. Murphy's mother called to ask him to turn the temperature knob to "defrost" before she got home from work that afternoon. As soon as he was off the phone, Murphy went to the refrigerator and turned the knob all the way to the right, as his mother told him. ("Or was it all the way to the left? It probably doesn't matter," he thought.)

Three hours later he heard a rumbling noise coming from the kitchen. Then a loud crash. He got there just in time to see a small glacier go through the kitchen wall, into the living room, and out the front door. The front door went with it, in fact.

Murphy didn't know what to do. He had never seen a glacier before—especially one that came out of a refrigerator. So he called the police.

"Hello, Officer! I'd like to report a runaway glacier."

"Sure you would. And my name's Santa Claus," said the police officer. "Tell me, what did this glacier look like?"

"Well, it's all white, and moving very fast for a glacier. It knocked down the door to our house and is heading down Spruce Street. Hurry, please!"

"I'm sure you must be mistaken," the police officer said, laughing. "We haven't had any glaciers around here for about five hundred thousand years. Now you'd better stop playing games, or you'll have something more than glaciers to worry about." And with that, the officer hung up.

Just then Murphy heard a siren and cars honking outside. He ran through what used to be the door and on down Spruce Street. The glacier was not hard to follow. It had become wider, until it was now a river of ice about ten feet high and twenty feet across. There were overturned cars and uprooted trees all along the street where it had passed. Near the intersection at Main Street, he could see two drivers angrily blowing their horns because the glacier wouldn't give them the right-of-way. There was also a big fire truck. Four fire fighters aimed a hose at the glacier, but it just kept right on moving.

For some reason the glacier took a right turn onto Main Street—maybe because the street was one-way. The glacier was getting bigger and bigger, and it pushed aside a whole row of parked cars as if they were toys. Passing by Mrs. Floradale's house, it dumped a few icebergs into her swimming pool.

Murphy noticed that an ice company truck had pulled up alongside the glacier. Men with air drills were cutting away chunks of ice and loading them into the truck, while nearby two of Murphy's friends were using ice picks to chip away ice for their lemon-ade stand. Murphy knew that something would have to be done soon. The glacier was chewing up the sidewalk along Main Street and was heading straight for the town hall.

He thought hard. He remembered what his teacher had said about the last ice age—how the huge glacier covering much of the northern part of the earth had started to melt when the average temperature be-came a few degrees warmer. Murphy suddenly knew just what to do.

He ran all the way back to his house. He jumped on the ice that was flowing out of the living room and, like a mountain climber, crawled toward the kitchen. "If I can just reach it in time," he thought. But while he crawled, the glacier kept moving in the opposite direction. For every inch that Murphy pushed forward, the ice pulled him backward by almost as much. So, it seemed like hours later when he finally reached the refrigerator. With all his might, he turned the temperature knob all the way in the other direction.

The glacier suddenly stopped. Outside he could hear people cheering.

Just then his mother came home. "Murphy, what happened?" she yelled as she stepped into the living room, where a small glacier now sat melting away.

"Oh, not much, Mom," said Murphy. "I'm just defrosting the refrigerator like you said."

The Spunky Princess

By Patricia Hubbard

Once upon a time there lived a spunky princess. The princess could pole-vault over her horse, Starburst, hit nine out of ten baskets through the regal hoop, and scale the castle walls up to the tower.

She was also beautiful. All the men in the kingdom wanted to marry her.

Royal law decreed that the king must choose his daughter's husband. Every Saturday young men lined up to ask for the princess's hand in marriage.

The problem was, this wasn't your run-of-the-mill, storybook kind of princess. She wanted to choose her own husband.

Now the king loved his daughter very much. He wanted her to be happy. So the king and the princess devised a plan.

The next Saturday the king sat on his purple throne, with Tiffany, his dog, at his feet. He asked the same question of each young man, "Why do you want to marry my daughter?"

"I have always wanted a wife with long, velvety hair," the first young man answered.

Then, while pretending to think, the king nudged Tiffany with his foot. The royal dog trotted over to the princess, who was hiding behind a gold satin curtain. She quickly wrote her opinion of the suitor on a note and placed it in Tiffany's mouth. The loyal dog carried her message to the king.

"No way," read the first note.

The king cleared his throat and said, "I'm sorry, young man, but you will not do."

The next suitor entered. "I want to marry your daughter because her skin looks as soft as white rose petals."

"Boring," wrote the princess.

Another young man declared, "I love her sapphire blue eyes."

"Forget it," the spunky princess scribbled.

And so it went, Saturday after Saturday, one rejected suitor after another.

Finally the princess said, "This is a waste of time."

The king looked wise. "When you find the right man, you will know he is special and you will live happily ever after," he said.

"That'll be the day," said the princess. She went outside to practice high dives into the moat.

One morning the princess woke up feeling odd. She looked in the mirror and saw a red splotchy pimple on her nose. There were two watery blisters on her ear. Some suspicious bumps dotted her cheeks. And those ugly spots itched!

She slid down the banister, scratching the top of her head. The king looked at her and proclaimed, "The princess has a royal case of the chicken pox."

After many days the court physician declared that the princess was no longer contagious. She felt fine, although her face was covered with crusty pink splotches.

The king gave the princess permission to ride Starburst. She galloped to her favorite meadow and was surprised to find a young man there. A silver stallion was drinking from the pond nearby.

"Hello," said the startled man. "I'm Prince Sterling, from a kingdom west of here. I hope it is all right to rest here for a while."

"Sure," the princess answered. "My dad and I run this kingdom. Your stallion is gorgeous."

They sat down on the soft grass. "I love Starburst more than all the gold in my father's vault," said the princess.

"I know just how you feel," answered the prince. "My horse is my most prized possession."

Just then a fish jumped in the pond. "Is it good fishing here?" asked the prince.

"You bet. My father and I fish for rainbow trout. I'm pretty good with a dry fly."

The prince was intrigued. "What a coincidence!" he said. "I love fishing."

The princess stood up. "I've got to head out so I can get home before the knights pull up the drawbridge. Besides," she continued, "I don't want to miss the banquet. I love to eat."

"What's your favorite food?" asked the prince.

The princess smiled mischievously. "Veggie Burgers at Lancelot's Ride-In," she said.

The prince helped her mount Starburst. "You aren't going to believe this. Veggies are my favorite, too," he said.

When she got home, the princess told her father about the fascinating prince. The king looked at his daughter's sparkling eyes and pockmarked face.

That night the torches burned late in the king's bedchamber. He paced back and forth, thinking about this unknown prince.

The next Saturday the first suitor in line at the castle door was Prince Sterling.

The king asked the standard question, "Why do you want to marry my daughter?"

"We seem to love the same things," Prince Sterling

replied. "She has a good sense of humor and a mind of her own. I like that in a princess."

The king studied him carefully. "What else?"

The prince took a deep breath. "I don't care if her face is terribly spotted. It is the beauty deep within her that I love."

The king smiled and gave Tiffany a gentle nudge. The royal dog disappeared behind the satin curtain.

Then the king began to laugh. He laughed until the purple throne was shaking. He laughed until the crystal chandeliers were swinging.

Tiffany returned with the message. "IT'S A DEAL!" read the note.

The king wiped his eyes and told the prince about the chicken pox. Then he said, "You have my permission to marry my daughter."

So the spunky princess and Prince Sterling were married in the meadow, mounted on their horses. The princess's face had regained its usual spotless beauty.

For their wedding feast they rode to the closest Lancelot's and had Veggie Burgers. And just as the king predicted, they lived happily ever after.

Otis Cranberry
and the Bubble Gum Record

By Jean E. Doyle

Otis Cranberry owned a copy of the *Book of Records*. Every day he read it. Some days he read a lot of it.

One day Otis had an idea. "I can break one of these records," he told himself. "Then they'll put my name in the *Book of Records*, too."

He thumbed through the book and stopped to read, *Girl blows bubble nineteen and one-quarter inches in diameter.* That didn't sound so great to Otis.

So Otis took some money from his bank, got his

best friend, Grover, and off they went to the store. Otis bought a dollar's worth of bubble gum.

On the way back home Otis put three whole pieces of bubble gum in his mouth at once and began to chew. He gave Grover a piece, too.

"How are we going to measure the bubble?" Grover wanted to know.

Otis stopped chewing for a moment. He said, "With a yardstick, of course. How else?"

They looked in the book again to check the record. *Girl blows bubble nineteen and one-quarter inches in diameter.* Grover asked, "What's a diameter?"

"From one side to the other," Otis mumbled, still chewing. "As if you were measuring right through the bubble."

His bubble gum was nice and soft now, just right for blowing. He pushed his tongue through it to make sure it would stretch well.

"Stand back," he warned Grover. "Here goes my first try."

Otis took three deep breaths, then began to blow slowly and carefully. A pink bubble began to form as Grover watched, yardstick in hand.

The first bubble burst before it was bigger than an orange. "That was just for practice," Otis told his friend. "I'm just getting warmed up."

Every time Otis blew a new bubble, it was a little bigger than the one before it. Soon he blew a bubble the size of a watermelon.

He clamped his lips tightly together and motioned frantically to Grover to measure the bubble. Grover held the yardstick up in front of the bubble. His eyes opened wide. "It's nineteen and one-quarter inches," he shouted. Otis let the bubble collapse.

"Why did you do that?" Grover demanded.

"I'm not out to *tie* the record," Otis reminded him. "I'm out to break it."

By now Otis's jaws were getting a little tired, but he would not give up. "I will not be a quitter," he reminded himself.

Twice more Otis blew large bubbles, but he wasn't satisfied when Grover measured them. "I can do better," he kept saying.

Finally Otis decided he was ready for the big try. Slowly he began to blow, and slowly a pink bubble began to grow. Grover stared with round eyes and open mouth as the bubble grew larger and larger.

Suddenly something began to tickle Otis's nose. He knew at once that he was going to have to sneeze. Was it possible that this great moment was about to be spoiled by an itch?

Otis kept blowing and the tickle grew worse. He could no longer keep the sneeze back. He clamped his front teeth to the part of the gum still left inside his mouth and sneezed loudly.

What happened next was a shock to both boys. Instead of bursting as they had expected, the huge bubble expanded with a lurch that popped it up and around Otis's head.

The next moment Otis was looking at his friend Grover from *inside the bubble*. There was plenty of air in there, so he felt no discomfort. When he realized where he was, he grinned—he didn't want to laugh out loud, for fear of breaking the bubble.

Grover was frantic. "Otis, do you think I should break it and set you free?" he yelled.

A faint but definite "No!" came from inside the bubble. "I like it in here."

Word spread quickly throughout the neighborhood. Soon Otis and Grover were surrounded by children of all ages and sizes.

A photographer heard about Otis and his head-bubble and came running with her camera. Otis and Grover proudly posed, surrounded by the admiring crowd.

After an hour of glory Otis began to feel funny. He was finding it harder to breathe and realized his bubble oxygen had just about been used up. Reluctantly he made a decision. He reached up and gave the enormous bubble a sharp poke. It popped, and Otis sat there with ragged pieces of gum hanging from his face and hair.

His mother was horrified when she saw him. "It will just have to wear off, I guess," she said.

Early the next morning Grover came running over to Otis's house, with a copy of the morning paper.

"We're famous!" he shouted. Otis looked at the

paper. There was a photograph of him grinning out from his huge bubble with the words BOY BLOWS BIGGEST BUBBLE IN TOWN printed under it. But because his head had been inside it, Otis figured the *Book of Records* wouldn't let it count.

Later the photographer came to Otis's house and handed him a ten-dollar bill. "The newspaper paid me for my photograph," she explained. "Here's a share of it for you."

Otis was pleased. "Well," he said slowly, "It isn't the *Book of Records,* but it's a start."

He reached over and picked up his well-worn book. "Now I can buy a new copy. And I can start making plans for my next try at a world record."

When You Wish upon a Rhino

By Margaret Springer

"I know just what you're wishing for," Tim said. "You're wishing for a puppy again."

"I am not!" said Clara. Why did brothers know everything? Every year on her birthday, Clara wished for a puppy.

Clara shut her eyes. Then she scrunched up her face. "Quiet," she said. "I'm wishing." She tried to think of something different. She whispered it inside herself, so her lips wouldn't move. "I wish . . . I wish for a rhinoceros."

"OK," said Clara. She blew out her candles with one breath. Her parents applauded.

That was Tuesday. On Thursday there was a knock at the door. Clara answered it. There on the doorstep stood a large, lumpy, dusty-looking rhinoceros.

"Are you Clara?" the rhinoceros asked in a tired voice. Clara nodded. Her eyes were wide, and her mouth was open.

"Well, here I am. The name's Reginald." The huge rhinoceros waddled into the living room. "I hope you don't mind if I sit down. It's a long walk from the zoo."

Reginald plunked himself onto the couch. The room shook, and a cloud of dust rose. "Well, what did you want me for?"

"You can't stay here!" said Clara.

"Whyever not? You wished for me, didn't you?"

"Yes, but my mom and dad will be home any minute and—"

"Great! Are there brothers and sisters, too?"

"My brother, Tim, is downstairs watching TV. But listen—"

"TV!" Reginald sat up suddenly. The couch springs sagged ominously beneath him. "I love TV! What's on? We hardly ever see it at the zoo."

Reginald started across the room. "Which way? Oh, I always wanted to live where there was a TV. I'm going to love this place. Say!" He looked toward the kitchen and sniffed. "Is there anything to eat? That long walk gave me an appetite."

Clara sighed. "What do rhinoceroses eat?"

"Well, most rhinoceroses like bulbs and leaves and grasses, but I prefer potato chips and some pistachio ice cream. And soda pop. Do you have any of that?"

"Maybe," said Clara.

Reginald gave her a pleading look. He did seem hungry, so Clara found some food. The rhinoceros slurped and gobbled everything she brought him.

After a while Reginald burped. Then he yawned. He spread himself on the couch again. He shut his eyes. Soon Clara heard gigantic snores.

Clara tiptoed out of the living room. She raced downstairs.

Tim was propped on one elbow watching a science show.

"Tim, you've got to help me! That rhinoceros I wished for is sleeping upstairs in the living room and—"

"Shush!" said Tim. "I can't hear my program."

Clara stood in front of the TV. "Listen to me, Tim. It's important! There's a rhinoceros in the living room, and he has already eaten up all the potato chips and guzzled five cans of soda pop."

"You're kidding me," said Tim.

"I'm not kidding!" Clara said.

Tim snapped off the TV. They rushed up the stairs two at a time.

Reginald was sitting up, squinting at one of their

magazines. "Listen to this," he said. "Why did the bear chew up a dollar? Because it was his lunch money! Oh, that's so funny!" The whole house shook with the sound of Reginald's guffaws.

"Mr. Rhinoceros—" said Tim.

"Hello! The name's Reginald."

"Listen, Reginald. You've got to go back where you came from right away, before our mom and dad get home."

Reginald looked sad. "Why?"

"Because you can't live here," said Clara. "People live in houses. Rhinoceroses live in zoos, at least in our part of the world."

"Then why did you wish for me?"

"I made a mistake," Clara said.

"Oh. You made a mistake." Reginald's big body slumped, and he sighed. "OK," he said. "You made a mistake, and now I have to walk all the way back to the zoo."

A car was in the driveway. Mom and Dad were home.

"Quick!" shouted Clara. "This way!"

They shoved Reginald through the back door and out into the garden.

"Thanks for coming," said Clara breathlessly. "And stay out of the flower beds. I'll phone the zoo, so you can get a ride home."

"But I didn't watch any TV," Reginald wailed.

In the living room, Mom had just put down her

big briefcase. "Have you two had friends over?" she asked.

"One friend," said Clara. "Sort of."

"Well, you should clean up afterward. You know that."

Dad was in the kitchen. He had the radio on. "A rhinoceros got away from the zoo," he called. "They're looking all over for it."

"Kind of a big thing to lose," Mom said. "Oh, am I tired! I wish I had a magic wand and—"

"No!" shouted Tim.

"Don't wish for things," said Clara. "Not unless you really want them, Mom."

Mom looked from one to the other. "You two are sure acting strangely. Is everything OK?"

They both nodded and smiled.

"I've got to make a phone call," Clara said.

It was almost suppertime when Dad called them to a window. Clara could just see the back end of Reginald disappearing into the zookeeper's van.

"Think of that!" Mom said. "The missing rhinoceros was on our street all along!"

"That reminds me," said Clara. "We should go to the zoo some weekend. It has been ages since we went there." She looked at Tim.

"Great idea," said Tim. "We'll take a portable TV with us."

"A portable TV?" Dad said.

Clara nodded. "And potato chips and pistachio ice

cream and soda pop," she said, smiling. "And maybe even a big pile of magazines with jokes in them."

The Lost Whistle of Dooly O'Day

By Kay Jones

Dooly O'Day was an Irish boy who liked to whistle. Now this boy made the grandest sound that ever was heard in the whole village of Ballybankie. When Dooly started whistling, the cows gave the richest milk, the hens laid the biggest eggs, and the sheep grew the finest wool in all the countryside. And if there happened to be an argument among the neighbors, it was: "Get Dooly O'Day, quick! His whistling will soon put an end to the quarreling."

And so it did. Nobody could listen to that sweet music for long without a smile and a dance.

Then came a day that Dooly would always remember. It started out just fine as the boy marched down the road toward the village post office to buy stamps for his mother. Soon he saw three cows in a pasture and halted to whistle them a tune. A while later, after he had passed tiny Kerry's Pond, he saw something sparkly lying in the grass.

Dooly picked up the small thing. "'Tis a magic harp!" he cried. "I'll keep it to bring me good luck."

When at last he reached the post office, he saw a card in the window. Dooly read it twice: *Lost, one gold harp. If found, please leave on the tree stump beside Kerry's Pond.*

Quickly drawing the harp from his pocket, Dooly stared down at it. So the owner wanted it back—the leprechaun of Kerry's Pond.

After getting the stamps, Dooly turned toward home. It seemed no time at all before he saw the tree stump amid bush and bracken. He glanced here, he glanced there. Was the leprechaun somewhere nearby? Was he hunting for his harp? Dooly thrust his hand into his pocket and fingered the small thing. He stepped into the bracken. The next minute he stepped back on the road.

"No," he said, "I'll not return the harp. Finders keepers."

A short time later he saw the cows again and pursed his lips to give them a tune—but no tune came forth. He blew and he blew, but not a sound could he make.

"Arrah, I've lost my whistle!" cried Dooly O'Day. "Whatever shall I do without it?"

And it was not only Dooly O'Day who missed his whistle. The entire village of Ballybankie missed it. The cows' milk was no longer the richest anywhere in the green countryside. The hens' eggs were no longer the biggest. And so thin was the sheep's wool, that it was not worth the taking.

As for the neighbors, they started arguing for the least bit of a reason. And much to his own amaze-ment, Dooly suddenly found himself fighting with his best friend, Mike Muldoon. Rolling about the grass they were, in front of Dooly's house, punching and pummeling each other until Dooly's mother came running out.

"Enough is enough, boys," she shouted, pulling them apart. "Whatever's the matter that two good friends should be fighting like this? I can't think what has got into everybody lately. Folk arguing and fighting with one another all of a sudden. Come, Dooly, give us a tune to cheer us up."

Dooly shook his head. "There'll be no tunes from me. I've lost my whistle."

"Lost your whistle!" cried Mrs. O'Day. "Who ever heard of a boy losing his whistle? Mind you, find it soon, or we'll be in a sad way indeed."

Just one week later Dooly O'Day went back to the post office to mail his mother's letters. He took the long way round through Fiddler's Bog so he would not have to pass the tree stump and maybe see the leprechaun waiting for his harp. The card was still in the window, and new words had been added.

Dooly read it again. *Lost, one gold harp. If found, please leave on the tree stump by Kerry's Pond.* Then came the new words: *'Tis sad I am without my harp.*

"And 'tis sad I am without my whistle," said Dooly. "I must keep the harp to bring me luck. Maybe it will help me find my whistle."

After mailing the letters, Dooly turned toward home. And so lost in thought was he that his feet took him where they pleased—straight along the road to Kerry's Pond. Halfway there, he drew the harp from his pocket. While feasting his eyes upon it, he kept thinking of those new words on the card: *'Tis sad I am without my harp.*

Now that he knew how it felt to lose something precious, Dooly was beginning to understand the leprechaun's feelings. A while later he had another thought. Swift and clear it was, out of the blue. "Sure, I'd like to make the leprechaun happy again," he thought. "Then maybe I'd feel less sad myself."

And so it happened that when Dooly O'Day came to Kerry's Pond, he stepped into the bracken, marched himself over to the tree stump, and carefully laid the harp on top. Then he crouched down behind a thicket.

He had not long to wait. In three shakes of a cow's tail, he saw a figure no taller than a twig emerge from the grass. He was dressed all in green except for his cap which was flaming red. The small man climbed the stump and picked up the harp in both arms. Then he turned toward Dooly with a smile and a nod. The next moment he disappeared.

Dooly's heart was lighter when he straightened up. "I feel better for letting the harp go," he thought. "There's one less to be sad now."

He set off down the road and soon came to the three cows, who nodded a greeting. "If it's a tune you're wanting, you'll not get it from me," he told them sadly. "My whistle's still lost."

To prove it, Dooly pursed his lips and blew. Then, greatly to his astonishment, the air was suddenly filled with lovely trilling as pure and musical as the sound of a thrush.

The lost whistle of Dooly O'Day had come back! And it was no time at all before the whole village of Ballybankie knew it. Once again the cows gave the richest milk, the hens laid the biggest eggs, and the sheep grew the finest wool in all that green countryside. As for the neighbors, they were soon going about with happy smiles, for they knew Dooly O'Day was somewhere nearby, ready to whistle them a merry tune.

The Strange Adventures
of
Miss Peacock

By MaryEllen Uthlaut

In the dark, a single light beamed down the street. At 34 Pumpernickel Lane, Miss Priscilla Peacock peeked out her window.

The light came closer. How exciting! The light grew brighter. How delightful! It stopped at Miss Peacock's very house. How frightful!

"Who goes there?" shouted Miss Peacock through the screen. "Friend or foe?"

"Why, I'm a friend," answered a voice. "I'm the paper boy."

Wow! A boy made of paper! Miss Peacock's left ear began to wiggle. She imagined the boy, pasted together out of pink and black paper. But from the window she spied only a shadowy figure.

"Just a moment, Paper Boy," said Miss Peacock as she turned on a light and stepped onto her front porch.

Swat! The morning newspaper landed on her doormat. Down her front path slithered a fresh bicycle track. But the headlight and the boy had disappeared.

"My, my!" said Miss Peacock. "There are so many strange things in the world, and I always seem to miss them. I am too slow."

Miss Peacock *did* walk more slowly than most people. But there was another reason that she missed seeing things. Miss Peacock never left her house on Pumpernickel Lane. When she read about something strange, Miss Peacock formed a picture of it in her mind, but she never, ever went to see it.

Once Miss Peacock read about a starfish. "A fish made of stars!" she said. "How beautiful it must be."

Once she read an advertisement for a barn dance. "Isn't it wonderful?" she whispered. "Nowadays even barns can dance."

Lately, though, Miss Peacock had grown tired of imagining.

"Just once in my life, I would like to actually *see* something strange," she said to herself. "Perhaps today I'll do that!" She picked up her newspaper and went inside.

Miss Peacock had gone no farther than the front page when she found a strange news item. It was about rockslides.

"What will they think of next?" said Miss Peacock. When she was young, slides were used by boys and girls. They were *never* used by rocks. Unfortunately, the rockslides were too far away to visit.

On page 17-B, however, was a very strange advertisement. GIANT FURNITURE SALE, it read.

"My, my!" said Miss Peacock. "What fun it would be to see a bed or a chair big enough for a giant. Why, a giant just might be shopping there, too."

Miss Peacock's left ear began to wiggle. At the bottom of the advertisement was the address of the shop: 78 Pumpernickel Lane. The GIANT FURNI-TURE SALE was right down the street!

"I have never seen giant furniture," said Miss Peacock. "I have never seen a giant. I am going." Taking her giant-sized shopping bag in case she wanted to buy something, off went Miss Peacock.

The furniture shop was crowded. Miss Peacock passed tables and chairs, beds and dressers, lamps and sofas. She saw more people than she had ever seen before. She stared until her eyes felt as big as baseballs. She walked until her swollen ankles felt as big as watermelons.

But Miss Peacock didn't see one piece of giant-sized furniture, or one giant shopper.

"Yoo-hoo! Manager!" shouted Miss Peacock.

A tall man with a mustache rushed over. On his coat was a button that read MANAGER OF THE MONTH.

"Sir!" demanded Miss Peacock. "I came to see the giant furniture you advertised." She shook the newspaper in the manager's face.

The manager of the month looked bewildered. "Madam," he said, "in our furniture shop we are having a GIANT SALE."

"Oh! A sale on giants?" Miss Peacock's left ear practically turned a somersault. She had wanted to see giant furniture. But how exciting it would be to see a real giant!

"Where are your giants, then?" she asked.

The manager rubbed his mustache. With a handkerchief, he mopped his forehead.

"I'm sorry, Madam," he said. "We are fresh out."

She was too late again. Miss Peacock shook her head. She was too slow after all. And her feet were sore. She never should have left her house.

Just then, Miss Peacock's *right* ear began to wiggle. She noticed a sign hanging on one of the bunk beds—a sign so small she had almost missed it.

ALL SHOPLIFTERS WILL BE ARRESTED, it said.

"Manager?" Miss Peacock pointed to the sign. "Would you arrest a giant?" Who else, she thought, would be strong enough to lift an entire shop?

"If he were a shoplifter, Madam, we would arrest him," the manager replied.

Miss Peacock stared at the tiny sign. Why, it must be a very powerful sign! Hadn't it scared every giant in town away from the furniture shop? And she, Miss Priscilla Peacock, had seen it with her very own eyes. Surely such a sign was worth leaving home to see.

"There are strange things in this world," Miss Peacock observed. The manager quite agreed.

As she turned to leave, Miss Peacock noticed the button on the manager's coat. Her left ear twitched. How, she wondered, had he ever become the manager of an entire month?

But when she turned back to ask, she saw the manager running out the back door.

"How strange," Miss Peacock said to herself. "He looks as if he has seen a giant!" She began to walk home on her tender feet. Tomorrow would be soon enough, she decided, to start her next adventure.

BURIED TREASURE

By Juanita Barrett Friedrichs

DANGER

NO ADMITTANCE
KEEP OUT, $50 FINE
VIOLATORS WILL BE
TOWED AWAY

In a normal family, putting up a sign like that should give you some privacy. But my family isn't normal. They're clowns. *Circus* clowns. My great-grandfather Wilhelm started it all, juggling double-scoop ice-cream cones when he was six. My parents call their act "Loopy Lou and Bashful Betty." My three brothers and three sisters are clowns, too. The whole family's a little unusual.

Except me. I am *not* a clown. No thanks. I'm the logical, serious, intelligent type. There has to be at least one in every family. The future of civilization depends on it.

I never start a project unless it's sensible and worthwhile. Like *Digging for Treasure in Your Own Backyard*. That's a book I just read. It sounded like a good idea.

So I got the shovel and put up my sign. I'll start digging between these two apple trees—for shade if the sun gets hot. That's logical thinking.

My mom's clothesline runs between the two trees, but she always washes on Saturday and this is only Tuesday. I figure by Saturday we'll all be million-aires and she can send out the wash.

The first day of my project is fairly peaceful. I'm the only one at home. Everyone else is rehearsing, except my father. He's busy dreaming up new acts for next year's circus season.

I dig down through Level One, and there isn't any treasure. But there sure are lots of worms. The news travels fast. Soon I'm running a wormburger restau-rant for all the birds in town.

Day Two begins in a promising way. Right off,

my shovel hits something that goes clang. I reach down for it. Visions of precious jewels and gold coins dance in my head. . . .

The label on the can says *Kute Kitty Kat Food*. What's that doing in Level Two? Oh, I know. It's my sister Daisy's week to empty the garbage. Her nickname is Lazy Daisy. I'd better add NO DUMPING to my sign.

Our dog, Jigger, decides to be my assistant. He smells last night's chicken bones. A lot of dirt flies out of Level Two, plus a lot of other stuff—ice-cream sticks, broken plastic spoons, banana peels.

You won't believe Day Three. Digging for treasure requires concentration. Try doing it while somebody practices walking a tightrope over your head. I have *two* somebodies—my sisters Cookie and Tizzie. There they are, teetering around on my mom's clothesline, one at each end.

"I got here first."

"No, I did."

"Wait your turn."

"Here I come. Get out of my way!"

They meet in the middle.

"Some treasure," I mutter as I shovel them out of Level Three.

Day Four. Level Four isn't any better. My kid brothers, Willy and Nilly, show up in their horse costume. Willy is the front end of the horse, and Nilly is the back end. They're practicing their zig-zag gag. When Willy turns right, Nilly turns left. After a while they come unfastened. Willy zigs off and leaves Nilly to zag around by himself, crashing into things. Pretty boring act. Until—you guessed it—the treasure hole is starting to get crowded again.

I hoist Nilly out by the tail.

By Day Five I'm desperate. Laundry day! I dig faster.

Bang! I hit something hard with my shovel. A water pipe. Within minutes we have a swimming pool in our backyard. Thinking fast, as I always do in emergencies, I add NO LIFEGUARD ON DUTY to my sign.

That doesn't bother my big brother, Jergen. He comes out of the basement carrying a raft he has been building out of old skateboards.

"Got to see if she floats," he pants as he and the raft shove off from shore.

Here comes my mom with a big load of laundry. "Hang this up for me, please," she says.

She doesn't seem to notice the pool, because she mutters, "No water," and hurries back into the house.

I have to borrow Jergen's raft in order to hang the laundry. It isn't easy, especially with Cookie and Tizzie up there on the line practicing and complaining about the clothespins being in their way.

Willy and Nilly show up—still in their horse costume—and decide to climb the tree to get apples. Well, that makes sense. Everyone knows horses love apples.

The racket's deafening, with Jigger running around and around the pool barking and all the neighborhood birds flying around squawking about their restaurant being flooded.

Then my father arrives. He's muttering to himself. Uh-oh.

"Knocked my brains out all week and still haven't thought of a new clown act. Now the plumbing breaks down."

"Dad, I can explain."

By the time my explanation gets to Level Five, my father is doing cartwheels all over the yard, just like his old self.

"But, Dad, I didn't *find* any treasure."

"Son, you just created the most terrific clown act the circus has ever known! I call that TREASURE! You're going to be the star—the greatest clown of them all!"

There goes the future of civilization, I'm thinking to myself as I practice a double somersault on Jergen's raft.

The Dragon That Munched

By Suzanne Burgoyne

"Roger!" his mother called up the stairs. "Have you finished your homework?"

"I wish," said Roger to Dragon, "there was no such word as homework."

Actually, Roger didn't say that. He typed it on Dragon's keyboard. Dragon was a computer. A new, hush-hush, experimental model computer that Roger's dad (a very important scientist) was working on. Roger wasn't supposed to be playing with

Dragon, of course. But his friend Charlie was a computer whiz, so Roger needed to practice to keep up.

The prompt DO NEXT? appeared in green letters on Dragon's monitor.

Roger was getting a headache from concentrating so hard. Also, he was hungry.

EAT, he typed.

EAT WHAT? replied Dragon.

COOKIE, typed Roger.

YUM, printed Dragon. THANK YOU.

Roger turned off Dragon and went down to the kitchen. "Mom," he said, "may I have a nibble-fritz?"

"What?" said his mother.

"I said, I'd like a chompsickle."

"What?"

No matter how hard Roger tried, he couldn't say the word *cookie*. Finally, he drew a picture.

"Ah," said Mother, "I know what you want." She handed him an orange.

Roger was hungry, so he ate the orange. Actually, it tasted pretty good. But it wasn't a cookie.

Roger went back upstairs to Dragon.

He typed, DID YOU EAT THE WORD—Roger discovered he couldn't type *cookie,* either— NUMMIEWAT?

YUM, printed Dragon. EAT NEXT?

Roger thought for a moment. Slowly, he typed into the computer, HOMEWORK.

YUM, said Dragon. EAT NEXT?

"Roger!" his mother called up the stairs. "Have you finished your thinkdoodle?"

"I'm doing it now, Mom," he yelled. He went to the phone and called his friend Charlie.

"Hey, Charlie, what are you doing?"

"I'm doing my memorpickle."

"That's what I thought," said Roger. "It can wait. Come over here. I've got something to show you."

Since Charlie lived next door, it wasn't long before he was standing next to Roger, blinking at Dragon's screen. "A computer that eats words? And after Dragon eats a word, nobody can say it? Hmm," he muttered. "There are number-crunching programs. But a program that munches words is something new. What are you going to do?"

"Well," said Roger, "I was thinking of all the words I could feed to Dragon. Words I'd like to get rid of, like *karate lessons*. I mean, my parents couldn't make me go if they couldn't say it, right?"

"I see what you mean," Charlie said. "But your vision is limited. Think big."

Before Roger could stop him, Charlie leaned over and typed NUCLEAR MISSILE after Dragon's EAT NEXT? prompt.

YUM, said Dragon. THANK YOU. EAT NEXT?

"Was that such a good idea?" asked Roger.

For some reason Roger wasn't very hungry for supper that night.

"Would you like a tumtickle for dessert?" his mother asked.

Roger shook his head. He hurried to wash the dishes so he could watch the evening news.

"And the crisis of the hour," the newscaster was saying, "is the breakdown in the arms negotiation talks. At the special session tonight, negotiators on both sides found themselves unable to pronounce the words *bumbledy boomdoom*."

Onto the screen flashed a frenzied scene. Men and women in dark suits shook their fists at one another across a long table.

Roger ran for the phone. "Charlie," he whispered, "get over here. Fast. We're in trouble."

Roger waited for Charlie to arrive before switching on Dragon.

HELLO, flashed Dragon's screen. EAT NEXT?

"What do we do?" Roger demanded. "We've got to get him to give the words back."

Another EAT NEXT? prompt flashed impatiently on the screen.

"Greedy, isn't it?" observed Charlie.

Suddenly Roger sat down at the keyboard and began typing.

"What are you doing?" Charlie asked.

CHOCOLATE FUDGE CAKE, typed Roger frantically. PISTACHIO ICE CREAM. LICORICE STICKS.

"Stop!" cried Charlie. "Not ticklish fix!"

YUM, printed Dragon. YUM. YUM.

ROOT BEER FLOAT, Roger typed. PEANUT-BUTTER-AND-JELLY SANDWICH. BUTTERED POPCORN.

YUM, YUM, YUM, said Dragon.

Charlie collapsed, blinking, into a chair. Roger's fingers were sweaty on the keyboard. He sure hoped this would work.

BANANA SPLIT. COCONUT DOUGHNUT. PIZZA WITH ANCHOVIES.

YUM, printed Dragon. YUM. All at once his letters flickered, like a hiccup. YUK.

Dragon's monitor suddenly filled with words, spewing across the screen faster than Roger could read them. Roger took a deep breath and crossed his fingers. "Cookie," he said.

"How did you do that?" Charlie asked.

Roger shrugged. "I just remembered what happened to *me* one time when I ate a lot of that stuff."

"You made Dragon upchuck all the words? By feeding him all that stuff?" Charlie blinked in disgust. "Yuk."

"Roger!" his mother called up the stairs. "Have you finished your homework?"

Roger thought those were the most wonderful words he'd ever heard.

Troubles with Kites and Bubbles

By Elaine Pageler

The wind whistled through the trees. I grabbed my kite and raced for the door.

"Hold it, Marty," Mom called. "Aunt Susan is coming over today, and I want you to entertain your cousin Bubbles."

I skidded to a stop. "Mom, Bubbles is a pain!"

"Bubbles is a sweet little girl," she answered.

Ha! My five-year-old cousin is about as sweet as a jar of dill pickles! But saying this to Mom would

93

only make things worse. So I said, "Look at this super, windy day. Why did you buy me that new kite if you didn't want me to fly it!"

"Take Bubbles with you. She can fly your old red kite," Mom replied.

An hour later Bubbles and I slammed our back-yard gate and headed up the hill behind my house. We ran smack into Mr. York, my neighbor. He was walking Touser, the smallest dog I've ever seen.

"So you're flying kites," said Mr. York. "I suppose you'll get them tangled in my apple tree again."

"No, sir, that was last year. I know how to fly kites this year," I answered.

Both of us ignored Bubbles, who was pretending to be a bullfighter. She shook my red kite in front of the dog's nose, danced around, and flashed the kite at him again. He growled, but fortunately Mr. York had his angry dog on a leash.

When we got to the top of the hill, I launched Bubbles's kite first. "It's easy. Just hold this ball of string in your hand," I told her.

"Yes, Marty," she said, a little too sweetly.

I turned to my kite. Up it went, dipping and then soaring, higher and higher. It was a black dot in the sky when I heard Bubbles's voice. "Help, Marty!"

Bubbles was turning somersaults. Her kite string was wound around several tall weeds.

"Oh, all right," I muttered. "Come here, and hold my kite reel."

It took a few minutes to free her line. I glanced up and saw Bubbles chasing after a butterfly. "Where's my reel?" I yelled.

Bubbles ran over and took her kite string. "It's over there," she answered, pointing at a rock.

Just then, a gust of wind tore the string free. My kite was loose! I made a dive, but it moved faster than I did. By the time I picked myself up, the reel was hurtling down the hill. I chased after it, and Bubbles followed. Another strong gust of wind lifted the reel off the ground. It landed on Mr. York's garage.

"Don't let your kite get away," I yelled at Bubbles. Glancing back, I saw the ball of string drop from her hand and tangle around a fence post.

I turned my attention to the line rising from the garage. There was a rake leaning against the wall. "Good," I said, heaving a sigh of relief. "I'll be able to pull it off without bothering Mr. York."

Slowly, I raked the line over to the side. In another minute, the reel would drop into my hand. Just then, Bubbles appeared above me. "Hi, Marty," she said.

"How did you get up on the roof?" I cried.

Bubbles grinned. "I climbed a tree." She grabbed the reel and yelled, "Catch!" Naturally, her aim was bad, and she missed me by a mile.

At the sound of her voice, Touser came racing into the backyard. He and the kite reel reached the same spot at the same time. It was at this exact minute that a big gust of wind sent my reel ripping toward the house with Touser right behind.

"Touser, leave that alone!" I yelled, racing after him. I ignored Bubbles, who started hollering about being scared to come down from the apple tree.

By now, little Touser had all four feet knocked out from under him. Still, he seemed to be sliding forward. I saw my kite line above his head. "Oh, no!" I cried. "My kite string is hooked on his collar!"

Mr. York came outside. "Marty, is your kite caught in my apple tree again?" he asked.

"No, sir," I answered. "Your dog is flying my kite. It's Bubbles who's caught in the apple tree."

I made a grab for Touser, who was now doing a bucking bronco act. He raced around me, and the string wrapped around my feet. Crash! The dog, the kite reel, and I hit the ground together.

Touser insisted on licking my face as I untangled him and reeled in my kite. Meanwhile, Mr. York brought his ladder and helped Bubbles down. She came running toward me with an apple in each hand.

"Kite flying is fun!" she sang.

I snatched Bubbles's hand, gathered my kites, and started home.

Bubbles skipped along at my side. "What should we play next time, Marty?"

"Checkers," I answered.

"Oh, goody!" she said with a giggle.

Something about her grin warned me that Bubbles could turn even checkers into a dangerous game.